T0365374

The ADVENTURES of BIBOLE, RIVOL and MICHELLE

Kidnapped, Part One

BRIAN FUJIKAWA

Illustrations by **Gil Balbuena Jr.**

Acknowledgments

I would like to thank and dedicate these books to my loving daughter.

Daisy K. McCasland Stuart, for without her and her ideas, these books would have never been. Daisy, I love you to the moon and back! You're the best daughter any father can ever have.

Thanks to my dearest friends Gene and Allyson Yamagata. Without their support, this book would have just been a thought. I thank you with all my heart.

For every book sold, a portion will go to nurturing Lifestyles Inc. for their ever support of families and children in need. We thank Paul and Mary Padlak. MPP, OM, CHT, IACT.

May these books reach out to children who are looking for a great adventure.

Order this book online at www.trafford.com
or email orders@trafford.com

Most Trafford titles are also available at major online book retailers.

Illustrations by Gil Balbuena Jr.

Print information available on the last page.

ISBN: 978-1-4907-6140-4 (sc)
978-1-4907-6139-8 (e)

Library of Congress Control Number: 2015909724

Trafford PUBLISHING® www.trafford.com
North America & international
toll-free: 1 888 232 4444 (USA & Canada)
fax: 812 355 4082

Once upon a time, in a forest not far from where you live, stood a large oak tree. At the bottom of this oak tree was a little red door. Behind this door lived a family of mice: Bibole, the son; Rivol, the father; and Michelle, the mother.

It was a cloudy day in autumn when all the animals in the forest were helping one another prepare for the long winter. While the parents were out gathering the last of the nuts and berries that had fallen or still remained on the bushes close to the ground, the children of the forest were doing what they did best—playing their favorite game of tag-you're-it and hide-and-seek. From the sky, the forest looked like it was on fire; and the leaves were a beautiful color of red, yellow, and gold. As the leaves fell to the ground, the young ones would make piles of leaves; then as all children would do, both human and animal alike, they would run and jump in the piles of leaves, laughing as hard as they could. Daisy K, Bibole's best friend, would play hide-and-seek with them. She always knew where they were hiding but pretended not to.

She would say, "I wonder where they could be?" She could hear them snicker in the leaves, would walk past them, then suddenly turning quickly, would run and jump into the waiting pile. As the leaves exploded into the air and slowly floating back down to the ground, Daisy would say, "I see you!" and Bibole and his friends would then jump on Daisy and tickle her until she shouted out "I GIVE UP!" As their laughter faded to a pleasant sigh, they would all then lie there quietly for a moment, enjoying the cool breeze that made the leaves slowly dance in the air, covering their bodies like a warm blanket so that once again they became invisible to all who walked the forest.

Of course, it wasn't long before all were giggling, and the forest would then come alive with laughter as if there was a written rule somewhere that say all children of every kind must not be serious for no more than a minute. As the autumn day slowly came to an end, the clouds would find a resting spot for the night and gather their friends to settle down for the evening. Snuggling together like fluffy sheep, the clouds picked the forest trees to use as their bed to settle in for the cold night. When the clouds did so, the darkness fell onto the forest faster than usual. While Daisy and her friends played their favorite games, they didn't notice the clouds selfishly stoking the evening sun, and darkness soon began to cover the forest like a blanket.

Then out from nowhere, a loving voice shouted out from deep within the forest, "Hurman! It's time to go home. The moon is round, and you know what that means." "Yes, Mother," Hurman sadly replied. Hurman stared at his friends with a look that let them know he wasn't ready to have the games end just yet. For Hurman, this wasn't just another day coming to an end. The moon was round and, as Daisy called it, is the full moon. It was no longer a secret to the forest; all who lived there knew it was a night of the weremouse. A night where their little friend would no longer be little. Now it was time for the littlest mouse in the forest to go home—home where he would stay locked in his room until the sun showed its warm face the next morning.

We watched Hurman walk away, his head drooping down like he just lost his best friend and with hands in his pockets, Hurman started walking in the direction he knew would take the longest to get home. The gang knew this was a hard time for Hurman. It always seemed the full moon came at the most unwelcomed time, a time when Hurman and his friends were having the most fun. Not wanting Hurman to feel bad, Daisy spoke up, saying, "It's getting late for me too. I'll see you all tomorrow." Bibole and the rest of the gang knew what Daisy was doing, so they all pretended and said the same thing. "Yeah, we're tired too." Bonny, the bunny, and Marsell even pretended to squeeze out a yawn. "Oh my! We didn't realize it was so late. Let's all go home. See you tomorrow!" As Hurman watched his friends scatter in different directions, a little smile found its way to his lips. As selfish as it might have been, Hurman was glad his friends stopped playing. *It's kind of like a close group of friends*, he thought. *If one has to stop playing, everyone else should stop playing also*. It was hard for Hurman to think that his friends would stay and keep playing while he had to go home and lock himself in his room.

Bibole and his friends knew this was a big deal to their little buddy, so instead of playing their favorite games, everyone decided to just split up and go back to asking their parents if they needed any help with the gathering of nuts and berries. Together, they did everything as a team. Turning to get on the trail leading home, Hurman heard Bibole yelling out, "Hey, buddy! Can I walk home with you?" Hurman smiled a little smile and said, "That would be great." Not knowing if Bibole truly understood what was already in the process of unfolding, possibly right in front of his very eyes, Hurman asked, "Aren't you afraid of me changing into the weremouse? You know it's going to happen, remember? That's why I have to go home early. Bibole, I don't want you to be scared, but I can feel the change starting to happen. Look!" As Bibole slowly turned and looked, Bibole could see the hair on Hurman's arms and legs getting longer. Bibole didn't know what to say, so he just spoke from his heart. "We're friends, right? I know you'd never hurt me, and besides, the clouds are covering up the moon. You can't completely change unless the moon is in full sight." "I know," Hurman said, "but it's like my body doesn't want to listen. I can feel the change wanting to happen."

Walking down the path to Hurman's house, Hurman would stop and take a deep breath from his inhaler. "Are you sure you're okay?" Bibole would ask whenever they stopped. Hurman put his head down and rubbed his eyes. As he did so, he took his glasses off and put them in his pocket. Bibole was starting to get a little nervous. "Why are you taking your glasses off? You know you can't see a thing without them." Hurman kept rubbing his eyes. "You know, it's funny. Every time I start to change and my eyes get bloodred, I can see everything! The darker it gets, the better I can see. I just wish they would stop burning." Bibole's curiosity was getting the better of him. "Can I see them? Can I see the color of your eyes?" Hurman slowly turned and looked straight into Bibole's eyes. Bibole couldn't stop staring at them. "You have wolf's eyes! They are bloodred too!" All Bibole could say was "This is so AWESOME!" Bibole saw how uncomfortable Hurman was. Then he realized he needed to be more of a friend to Hurman than ever before.

"I'm sorry, does it still hurt? Can I do anything to make it better?" Hurman tried to smiled and then said, "It will be okay. It'll be dark soon, and I'll be able to see everything." As the two friends got closer to Hurman's house, Hurman fell to the ground once again, clutching his belly. "Are you okay? What can I do? What do you need, Hurman? Just tell me!" Hurman rolled over and said in a low growl, "I NEED TO FEED!" Bibole thought, *Oh boy, it's time. Here it comes.* But the change didn't happen. The clouds were too thick in the sky. "Don't worry, Hurman. I'll get you home." It was getting darker by the minute, and soon, Bibole wouldn't be able to see anything. But on the other hand, Hurman would be able to see like it is noonday. Bibole told Hurman, "It's getting dark, buddy. I'm having trouble seeing." Hurman told Bibole to hold on to his tail. As Bibole grabbed on, Hurman said, "You're going to have to just trust me." Bibole gave a sheepish grin and said, "I trust you. We're friends, right?"

With Bibole holding on to Hurman's tail as they walked through the forest, climbing up and over the roots of the trees, Hurman suddenly pulled Bibole to the ground. Hiding behind a large root, Hurman put his finger to his lips and made the sound, "Sh!" Bibole curiously said, "What's going on?" Hurman said with a voice of urgency, "You're not going to believe what I just saw!" Bibole quickly stood up and tried to focus and see what Hurman was looking at. Hurman quickly pulled Bibole down to the ground with a quick tug of Bibole's tail "Hey! What's going on? What's the big idea?" "Sh!" Hurman said again, this time with a little more urgency. "You're not going to believe what's out there." Bibole started to get a little frustrated. "Well, tell me. What did you see?" "I saw the three evil rats: Dr. No, Dr. Do Evil, and Dr. Feel Bad! They're here in our part of the forest!" Bibole replied, "I don't know what the big deal is. The faster they get back to their side of the forest, the better." Hurman, now in a state of panic, said, "The big deal is . . . they have your mom and dad tied up and gagged and thrown over their shoulders!" "WHAT?" Bibole yelled out. "I've got to save them!"

Bibole tried to climb over the root that they were hiding behind. Hurman once again pulled Bibole to the ground with a hard tug of his tail. "Let me go! Let me go!" Hurman covered Bibole's mouth with his hand. "Sh! You can't help them if you're caught too. We need a plan. If they see or hear us, we're done." Bibole and Hurman sat and thought for a short while. Even though Bibole wanted to run out there, he knew Hurman was right. So he stopped, calmed himself down, and took a deep breath. As they sat and calmed themselves, Bibole thought for a moment, then asked, "Which way were they going?" "They were going in the direction of your house. Why?" "My house! That's it! I've got an idea!" Bibole grabbed Hurman by his shoulders and then said, "I need you to get me to my house as fast as your feet can run. When we get there, you can have all the blueberries your heart desires." Hurman, very happy to hear this because he was starving, jumped up and said, "What are we waiting for? Let's go!"

When they arrived at the house, Hurman made a beeline for the refrigerator door. When he opened the door, he couldn't believe his eyes. There from top to bottom were blueberries. Hurman started stuffing his face as fast as he could. He was like a bear getting ready for winter. Hurman's face looked like a chipmunk's, cheeks bulging, because he couldn't get those berries into his mouth fast enough. Bibole watched for a moment, then under his breath, said, "That's just gross!" Then Bibole ran quickly to his parent's room and straight to the bookshelf, talking to himself, saying, "Which book is it? I know it's a green book. Come on, green book. Green, green, green. There it is!" The book read *Of Mice and Men*. Bibole then pulled the book toward him like a lever. The bookshelf rolled back, revealing three poles that seemed to disappear into a dark pit. Bibole grabbed on to one of the poles. This time not closing his eyes, he slid down into the darkness. As his feet hit the ground, without hesitation, he ran and turned on the lights. One by one, the lights went on, showing the entire cave with all its magical and mysterious things that lay waiting to be used by its rightful owners.

Still amazed that this cave was built by his parents, Bibole shook his head and thought, *I just need to get things we're going to need to help us save my parents.* As Bibole looked around, the first thing he grabbed was the ninja outfit. Then he grabbed two black backpacks. He knew the packs were full of great and useful things. Bibole could explain pretty much everything in the cave. The only thing he couldn't explain was the mystical ninja outfits. They had great and unexplainable powers. When he put one on, it was like magic. He would instantly know kung fu. The other things that were in the pack just made his quest so much easier. Bibole grabbed the other thing, which is the night-vision goggles, because he knew without them, all the kung fu in the world would be useless unless he used the night-vision goggles. With these goggles, like Hurman, he too would have the gift of sight. The darkest of nights would seem like noonday.

Returning from the cave, entering the kitchen, Bibole saw a plump and satisfied little mouse propped up against the kitchen wall. "Are you ready to go?" Bibole asked. With a huge purple grin on his face, Hurman said, "I sure am!" Doing a double take, Hurman rubbed his eyes then took a long stare at Bibole. "What in the world are you wearing?" In the kitchen stood Bibole, dressed in a black ninja outfit, black backpack, helmet, and a pair of night-vision goggles. Handing a backpack to Hurman, not really knowing what to say, Bibole said, "We don't have time. I'll tell you about it in the morning." Opening the front door, turning to Hurman, Bibole said, "Let's go get my parents back." While running through the forest, Hurman had a couple of crazy thoughts on his mind. *Just a short while ago, Bibole was blind as a bat! Now he can see as clear as I can. What's up with that? And that ridiculous helmet and strange outfit, he looks like a bug with those goggles on!*

Climbing over tree roots and rocks, Hurman finally caught up to Bibole. "The evil rats have such a head start on us. How are we planning on catching up to them?" With a look of determination on his face, Bibole said, "Simple. We'll go where they won't look." Curious, but afraid to ask, Hurman did what he didn't want to do. Knowing he'd regret it, Hurman asked, "So where is this place they won't look?" Grinning from ear to ear, not saying a word, Bibole pointed straight up. Slowly, Hurman looked up. "I don't see anything, just clouds." Smiling, Bibole said, "That's right! The clouds will be our cover." "The clouds? Are you crazy? We're mice! And on some occasions, I'm a weremouse! Last time I checked, we don't fly! Do you know why we don't fly? Because we don't have wings!" Finally, Bibole yelled out, "Would you please stop yelling! Do you want everyone in the forest to know what my plan is? If the evil rats didn't know we were following them, they do now." Hurman quietly apologized. "I'm sorry, but it's not my fault. It's these darn clouds. You know my body wants to change into the weremouse, but the clouds won't let me. They keep blocking the moon. It's making me a little cranky. So I'm sorry, okay? Now I don't know what your great plan is, but you know I'm scared of heights, right? You know, nosebleeds. It's not pretty."

Grabbing Hurman by the shoulders, Bibole looked his friend square in the eyes and told him, "You're just going to have to trust me." Hurman shrugged. "Every time you say that, it makes me nervous." Finally arriving at their destination, Bibole turned to Hurman and said, "We're here." Standing in front of one of the larger trees in the forest, Hurman looked around. "What do you mean we're here?" Not speaking, Bibole turned and began to gently glide his hand over the bark of the tree. Finding its mark, Bibole did what he saw his mother do just once before. Pushing on the tree knot closest to his eye level just like before, a door slowly opened. "WHAT? WHEN? HOW?" Hurman couldn't believe what he was seeing. Sticking his head slowly into the doorway, Hurman looked up. Looking at Bibole with disbelieving eyes, Hurman then stared up the stairwell leading straight to the top. Knowing what Hurman would say, Bibole just said, "We don't have time. I'll tell you about it in the morning." Holding on to the rail, higher and higher Bibole and Hurman climbed. The closer they got to the top, the more the tree would sway. "I think I'm going to be sick!" Hanging his head over the rail, Hurman swore he was going to lose his dinner and throw up. Laughing out loud, Bibole told Hurman, "Don't feel bad. I did the same thing not too long ago." Finding out Bibole got sick also gave Hurman the extra confidence he needed to continue to the top. Sometimes when you find out your friends have weaknesses too, you then realize you're not as weak as you think.

At the top, Hurman asked, "Now what?" Bibole told his very nervous friend to hold on to the door's rim. Opening the door at the top was like sticking your head into a wind tunnel. On this particular night, the wind was a lot stronger than the last time Bibole made the attempt to fly. Nervous but determined, Bibole knew he couldn't let his friend Hurman see his fear. If he did, Bibole knew that's all it would take for Hurman to find an excuse to get off that swaying tree Hurman called a death trap and call it quits. Bibole needed Hurman, and it would have been so much harder without him. He also needed the weremouse. Trying to swallow because his mouth was too dry from fear and the constant blowing of the wind, Bibole stepped out onto the swaying branch that extended out over the forest and slowly walked his way out to the middle, the same middle where just a little while ago on the same branch, in the exact same spot, he thought his life was going to come to a crashing end.

Turning to flag his friend over to come join him, Bibole saw Hurman squeezing the handrail of the stairwell with all his might, trying his best not to move a muscle. Because the wind was screaming in his ears and its sound was like thunder, Bibole thought he had to scream across the branch so that Hurman could hear him. He yelled, "Come on, buddy! We have to hurry!" Shaking his head, Hurman managed to yell out the word no. In a state of panic, Hurman yelled out, "It's too high! I'm going to get a nosebleed!" Trying to be patient, Bibole, with two of his fingers pointed at his eyes, said, "Look at me, Hurman. Don't take your eyes off mine. We're friends, right? I'd never let anything bad happen to you. You're just going to have to trust me, buddy. I need you." Trying to be brave, getting down on all fours, Hurman crawled out onto the branch and over to Bibole.

Remembering what his mother, Michelle, did the first time he climbed out there, Bibole reached down and grabbed his friend by his backpack straps and lifted him up. Standing on his two feet, Hurman quickly reached into his pocket, pulled out his inhaler, and took a deep breath, eyes wide and looking at Bibole's face, not wanting to look anywhere else. Bibole explained to Hurman, "I want you to do exactly what I do." Not knowing if it was his keen weremouse senses tingling in his belly, Hurman knew for some strange reason Bibole was going to do something that went completely against everything Hurman believed in and stood for. And that was keeping his two little feet planted firmly on the ground. And yet there he was at the top of one of the tallest trees in the forest, swaying back and forth and holding on for dear life. Hurman was having cramps in his stomach, not really knowing if it was from the transformation that was trying to take place in his body or if it was from the simple fact that Hurman knew deep down in his gut what Bibole was about to make him do.

Hurman thought to himself, *Why else would we be up here? To have a better view, then climb back down? No such luck. But why jump? We'll just fall to the ground like two bird eggs falling from their nest. Two bird eggs ready to be scrambled when they go splat on the ground.* "This is nuts! Bibole! I can't do this! You're my friend, and I really like your parents, but that's not a good enough reason for me to jump off of a perfectly good tree and kill myself." Bibole, still holding on to Hurman by his backpack, shook his pack straps and yelled, "You're not going to fall, Hurman! In fact, we're going to do the impossible. We're going to fly!" Scared out of his mind for a brief moment, Hurman didn't notice the tree swaying back and forth. He didn't notice the wind blowing like it was coming from a wind tunnel. What he did notice, however, was the confident grin on Bibole's face as he broke the news to Hurman about his "what he thought was an excellent plan." Limp from fear, the only thing keeping Hurman from plummeting to the ground was Bibole's grip on Hurman's backpack as he shook him, snapping Hurman out of his state of shock, and slowly coming to, Hurman's eyes became focused.

Noticing the wind howling and the tree swaying and that outfit Bibole had on that Hurman thought made him look like a bug, Hurman cried out, "Why are you doing this to me? What did I ever do to you to make you want to torture me like this? You keep telling me we're friends, and yet here we are at the highest tree in the forest, getting ready to do something galactically stupid! Why do I have such a strong need to remind you once again, Bibole, this doesn't make me happy? I really don't like high places, Bibole, especially if you're talking about jumping!" Standing up to Bibole made Hurman feel pretty good. He knew it was the weremouse in him that gave him most of his courage. Then out of the blue, Hurman felt his weremouse instincts kick in. Stomach tingling, Hurman had the strongest urge to ask Bibole a question. A simple question, and yet, it took all his courage and strength to ask. "Bibole, how many times have you done this?" With a sheepish grin and a tiny voice of a whisper, Bibole said, "Once, kind of." Now, under any normal circumstance, Hurman wouldn't be able to hear Bibole's answer because of the wind and the fact that he whispered under his breath. But the fact that Hurman had some of his weremouse abilities made it very easy for him to hear a pin drop on the other side of the forest.

So what he heard came in loud and clear. "ONCE? ONCE? ONCE? KIND OF? What do you mean by 'kind of'?" Not wanting to lie, Bibole told him, "It almost killed me, okay? I didn't do it right the first time, so the wind took me for a long and really uncomfortable ride. The only thing that saved me from crashing into the rocks was my parents." Staring at Bibole with a look of horror on his face, wishing Bibole would have just lied to him about trying to fly only once before, Hurman yelled, "Would it have killed you to lie to me just this once? Couldn't you have said, 'Oh, I've done it a hundred times before. No big deal'? But NO! You had to play the honesty card. Give me one good reason why I shouldn't just turn around and leave you up here by yourself. Just one good reason!" Bibole stared at Hurman, finally saying, "Because if it were your parents, we'd be up here, and it would be me helping you." With a frown on his face, Hurman just said, "FINE . . . FINE! I'll help, but I don't have to like it! Just because I can turn into a weremouse doesn't mean our fears go away. In fact, they grow along with our bodies. So when I say I'm scared up here, multiply it by a GAZILLION!" Shaking his head, all Bibole could say was "Wow. Really? Really? With all that complaining, we could have been back eating blueberry pie with my parents! Are you done?"

Reaching into his pocket, Hurman pulled out his inhaler again, and taking a deep breath, Hurman nodded. He knew he said everything that had to be said. It was Bibole's feeling that sometimes you got to just listen when someone is complaining. Let them get it out of their system by talking about whatever it is that's scaring or bothering them. Sometimes with the proper guidance, we can learn to overcome our fears. The only reason Bibole pushed like he did was because his parents were involved. Any other time, they would have been too busy playing their favorite games. Standing side by side, Bibole nervous and Hurman scared out of his mind, they looked over the edge. Both friends looked at each other, counted to three, and then did the unthinkable. "One, two, three . . . GO!" Doing a perfect swan dive off the branch, Bibole and Hurman disappeared into the darkness below. Silence filled the forest for just a split second. Then shooting straight up into the sky like two jet fighter pilots, the forest, once silent, is now filled with the sounds of "YAHOO! This is AWESOME!" Laughter and the sounds of "YEEHAWS!" echoed, filling the dark forest and the air above.

Finally catching up, Bibole yelled over to Hurman, "Keep it down! We don't want the evil rats to know we're up here!" "Sorry! I just never thought I could feel so free! So alive! I never ever want to walk again for as long as I live!" While the two mice darted across the dark skies, Hurman, feeling so free, so alive, never wanting to walk again, forgot the main reason why they were up there in the first place. On the other hand, Bibole kept a watchful eye out for a sign of any movement down below. Knowing they had to be close, Bibole's night-vision goggles made all the difference in the world. If his parents were still alive, the night-vision goggles would help find them. The glasses worked simply by picking up any living thing's body heat. Looking for any signs of life on the ground, Bibole stopped paying attention to Hurman and his loop-the-loops he was masterfully accomplishing. "Look at me, Bibole! Look what I can do!" Carefully watching the ground, Bibole said without looking, "Yeah, that's just great." Mastering the loop-the-loops, now the corkscrew, Hurman felt more alive and more adventurous than ever before. "I feel like I can fly to the moon!" Busy looking for his parents, under his breath, Bibole said, "Yeah, let me know how that turns out." Then, like a lightbulb turning on in his head, Bibole's eyes widened. "THE MOON! Hurman . . . NO!" Darting upward, breaking through the clouds, Hurman saw a familiar sight. What looked like a billion holes poked in a blanket of night, the stars shone like glitter thrown across the evening skies.

For a moment, Hurman would forget. Forget about his curse. Forget he had another side to him that he didn't like. Forget with stars comes the moon. With the moon comes the weremouse! Shooting up through the clouds, wide-eyed, Bibole could see the look on his friend's face changing. It wasn't what Bibole expected. Bibole stared into the eyes of his changing friend. All he saw was the look of sadness and the look of a scared child growing across his friend's face. Above the clouds, Bibole reached out to grab his friend's hand. Bibole wanted his friend, if he was still in there, to know he didn't have to ever do this alone again. Fully changed to an adult weremouse, Hurman squeezed Bibole's hand to let him know he understood what Bibole was saying. A low growl came from deep down in the weremouse's throat. "Okay, buddy! Now that we understand one another, could you please let go of my hand? You're crushing my fingers! I hear bones snapping!" Quickly letting

Bibole's hand go, shaking his fingers to get the blood circulating again, Bibole could swear he could still hear bones snapping. "What is that sound? There it is again!" *Snap*! This time the sound got louder. In what seemed to be a second, Bibole put two and two together and realized he heard that sound once before.

It was a sound he didn't want to ever hear again. The last time he heard that sound, one of his wings broke off. Realizing the glider wings were not designed to hold a mouse five times its size or even five times its weight put both friends in a very serious position. A position where there was only one direction where this problem was heading. That direction was straight down. With a look of fear on both their faces, Bibole watched as the brace of the glider wing made its last snapping sound, and then it did what he already knew was going to happen. As the wings began to fall apart and started to flutter away like a butterfly, Bibole stared into the eyes of his friend, knowing full well this could be the end. The end of his longtime friendship with Hurman and his newfound friend, the weremouse. *How do I break the news to his family? How do I break the news to his friends and mine? This is my fault! I didn't have to drag him with me. He made it perfectly clear he didn't want to do this. But I was selfish! I needed the weremouse! I just wanted to save my family.* All these thoughts ran through Bibole's mind in a flash, watching the weremouse disappear into the clouds below. The weremouse didn't make a sound. All he did was stare at Bibole, never taking his eyes off him until he was gone, vanishing through the clouds like he was never there. But he was there. Thinking to himself, Bibole said, "That's my friend falling, and I've got to save him! Or at least die trying!"

Cutting through the clouds like a falcon, Bibole had one thought on his mind, *Hurman's not dying tonight!* Grabbing the weremouse by his tail, Bibole pulled with all his might. Realizing his wings couldn't hold him and the weremouse, Bibole's grip got even tighter. "I'm not letting go! No matter what!" Hearing the unmistakable sound of a snap let Bibole know it was time, time to let go—let go, or they both wouldn't be able to save anyone, including themselves. Still, he held on with all his strength. In the back of Bibole's mind, he quickly thought, *Sorry, Mom and Dad. Sorry I couldn't rescue you. I tried. I just wanted you to be proud of me. I wanted to be able to hear you say . . . "There goes our son! He saved us from the evil rats." Sorry I can't be a hero for you.* That's when it dawned on Bibole. *My wings, they should have been breaking apart into little pieces by now.* Trying to figure out the mystery of why his glider wings didn't turn into splinters, Bibole also realized the weremouse wasn't as heavy as he used to be. Looking down, a smile raced across Bibole's face. "Thank you, CLOUDS!" He had forgotten what it meant to the weremouse when there was no moon to be seen. "Hurman! You're back!" Slowly opening his eyes, not remembering what had happened for the last few minutes and being upside down because he was soaring through the air while Bibole held on to his tail, Hurman screamed out, "TREE!"

Looking up, Bibole didn't realize just how close they came to a very unhappy ending. It seemed they were just feet from the ground, and the two mice were flying just below the tree line and going a lot faster than expected. Weaving in and out of the way of the trees, doing the best he could with only one arm to steer while the other held on to a wiggling and screaming Hurman, they both did what was to be expected—they hit a tree. But before crashing into this very large tree, covering both eyes with his hands, Hurman grunted under his breath, "Oh boy, this is going to hurt!" Crashing into the tree that stood the tallest in that part of the forest, Bibole and Hurman came to an abrupt stop.

Falling, the two little mice seemed to have hit every branch on the way down. Grunting and groaning every time they hit a branch, Bibole and Hurman suddenly stopped. Slowly opening his eyes and trying to get them to focus, Bibole thought to himself, *Well, that wasn't too bad. In fact, our landing was pretty soft. For a second, I thought we landed on my bed.* With a little grin on Bibole's face, he thought, *Anytime you can walk away from an accident, it's a good day.* Bibole then sat up and looked around. Blurry eyed, his vision slowly came into focus. Turning his head, he could see Hurman still lying there motionless. Bibole quickly crawled over to his buddy's side. "Hurman! Are you alive? Speak to me!" Eyes still shut, Hurman slowly rolled over on his side and, in a sleepy groan, said, "Can I have another kiss on my cheek, Mother?" With a confused look on his face, Bibole mumbled under his breath, "Asleep, he's asleep. How can he sleep at a time like this?" With his eyes still shut, Hurman puckered up his lips, expecting a kiss from his loving mother. Looking at Hurman in disgust, leaning as far back as he could so as not to get kissed by Hurman, Bibole quickly replied, "You want a kiss? I'll give you a kiss!" Smacking Hurman in the back of his head with his hand made Hurman jump straight up in the air, yelling, "WHAT THE! WHO DID!" Looking at Bibole and rubbing the back of his head, Hurman realized what Bibole just did. "What was that for?" "Next time you try to kiss me, I'll give you another smack in the back of your head." Still rubbing his head with a confused look on his face, Bibole and Hurman started to examine where they had fallen and what made their landing so soft. "Feathers? We landed in a pile of feathers," Hurman giggled. "How lucky was that?"

Laughing and rolling in the soft feathers like a child playing in snow, Hurman quickly jumped up in the air, yelling, "Ouch! Something poked me! Pull it out! Pull it out!" Grabbing hold of the sharp object, Bibole pulled as hard as he could. Rubbing his backside still in pain and looking at Bibole, Hurman said, "Thanks." At any other time, Bibole would have been rolling on the ground laughing as hard as he could. But not this time. This time, Bibole's eyes were fixed on the sharp object that he held in his hand. A sharp object Bibole recognized. "What was that thing? It hurt!" Looking at Hurman, Bibole raised his hand and, in a loud whisper, "Stop! Don't move a muscle! Don't even breathe!" Frozen like a statue, Hurman watched as Bibole slowly walked over to him. "Why can't I move? More importantly, why can't I breathe?" Covering Hurman's mouth with his hand, Bibole whispered, "Sh!" Turning his head from side to side, looking all around where they stood, Bibole whispered, "We need to leave this place. We need to leave this place now!" "Why? What's that thing you pulled out of my butt?" Holding it up for Hurman to see, Bibole said, "I know what this is." "Okay, you've got a thorn in your hand." Shaking his head, Bibole said, "No! It's not a thorn. It's a tooth! A rat's tooth!" "Well, what's a rat's tooth doing here? Rats don't lose their teeth."

Cautiously looking around, Bibole said, "He didn't." With his left foot, Bibole slowly removed a layer of feathers out from under them, exposing a mixture of bones from different animals. "Oh man! Did we land on a graveyard?" Nodding his head, Bibole's reply was quick and cold. "Yes, the worst kind of graveyard." With a look of confusion on his face, Hurman shook his head. "Sometimes, I just don't understand you. What do you mean the worst kind of graveyard?" Bibole's answer sent chills up Hurman's spine. "In this particular graveyard, these animals weren't ready to die." Wrapping his hands around Hurman's mouth like a muzzle, Bibole calmly spoke, "Hurman, promise me you won't scream, panic, or throw up on me when I tell you this. Promise you'll stay calm like I'm calm." Wide-eyed and not being able to speak because Bibole's hands were still wrapped around his mouth, Hurman nodded. "Now take out your inhaler and take a deep breath." Letting go of Hurman's mouth, he took the deepest breath he could. Whispering, Hurman asked, "Where are we?"

Calmly and slowly speaking so as not to panic Hurman, Bibole said, "It seems we've landed in the middle of a nest." "WHAT!" Grabbing Hurman's mouth once again, Bibole whispered, "Sh!" Slowing removing his hands from Hurman's mouth, trying to be as quiet as possible and scared out of his mind, Hurman said, "Wha-wha-wha-what kind of nest?" "It appears we've landed in a barn owl's nest." Whispering as loud as he could, Hurman said, "BARN OWL! Shouldn't he be in a barn? That's why they're called *barn owls*. They live in a barn! This isn't a barn. It's a tree. He's not living up to his title! BARN OWL! That's cheating! He doesn't deserve the title BARN OWL! It's like a church mouse! Where does he live? IN A CHURCH! Hence the name CHURCH MOUSE! I can't take this anymore! Where's my inhaler? Where's my inhaler?" Bursting into tears, Hurman, for just a brief moment, would go a little crazy. Bibole, on the other hand, tried to keep his little friend from letting every living thing in the forest know they were there. The last thing they would want is a visit from something that would consider them to be a snack.

Diving on top of Hurman and holding his mouth shut, they crashed and rolled to the bottom of the feathered flooring of the nest. Hearing the clatter of old bones scattering and feathers quietly floating in the air like snowflakes on a winter's day, Bibole's attempt to keep Hurman quiet didn't go exactly as planned. Forgetting his glider wings were still extended, Bibole could hear the snapping and tearing of wood and cloth as they rolled. When the struggle for silence was over, what remained were two tattered-looking mice. Wings bent and torn, night-vision goggles crooked and half-off, and feathers sticking out of places in their clothes where once there were none. A sight, needless to say, that looked ridiculous. Huffing and puffing as they stood looking at one another, their hearts finally settling down at the same time the feathers did, Hurman and his weremouse instincts felt a cold chill rush through his belly. Not moving a muscle and just using his weremouse instincts, Hurman quietly whispered, "Something's wrong. I feel it."

Like two statues holding their breath, they waited and listened. The deafening sound of silence screamed across the forest. Bibole and Hurman could hear each other's heartbeats. Finally exhaling with a sigh of relief, hoping it was just his imagination running wild and not his weremouse abilities, Hurman looked at Bibole, saying, "I think the coast is clear. We need to get out of here." Turning and walking very carefully, trying to avoid making any more unnecessary sounds than the sounds they already made, Bibole and Hurman headed toward the rim of the nest. Have you ever heard the expression, "If it sounds too good to be true, it normally is"? Well, in this case, this was one of those times. Reaching the rim, Bibole and Hurman looked at each other, not believing they had actually made it. "We did it! How lucky can two buddies be?" Trying to keep their laughter down, knowing if there was an owl, their nervous laughter and every other sound they made in that nest should have alerted the owl by now. "Where was it? Did it move?" "Why are you trying to analyze why we're not being eaten? Let's just get out of here before it does come back." Hurman said with a cautious whisper, "My whole body is tingling," as Hurman gripped his belly. Looking at Hurman with a nervous glance, Bibole asked a question Hurman didn't want to answer at all. "You ever have the feeling you're being watched?" With his head down, Hurman just nodded his head and said with a quiet voice, "Yes."

Not satisfied with just a one-word answer, Bibole asked, "When?" Slowly looking into Bibole's eyes, Hurman whispered the word, "Now." Bibole's body froze alongside Hurman's, and he stared out into the dark forest, standing on the outer rim of the cemetery of a nest, waiting for their bones to be mingled in with the rest of the others who were also unwilling to be part of death's collection. Finally, Bibole and Hurman, with eyes closed tightly, slowly turned around. Blubbering, Hurman said as he tried to hold his tears back, "It's been great knowing you, Bibole." Trying his best to be brave, Bibole let out a sigh and said, "You too, my friend." Standing there in the silence, both mice waited for what seemed to take an eternity. Waiting for death to show itself in the form of an owl, an owl for some reason wouldn't show itself. As if they were being toyed with, studied, and examined. Then it happened. "Why don't you come out from where you're hiding! Are you scared? Come on! Show yourself! COWARD!" Bibole's eyes had a look of "What the heck are you doing? Are you crazy? Do you want to die?" "I can't take this anymore. He's toying with us, Bibole! If he thinks I'm going to be easy to eat, well, he's got another thing coming." Screaming at the top of his voice, Hurman added, "I'm part weremouse, you know! I'll make sure you choke on me! You'll have the worst tummyache ever! Come on! Show yourself!"

    Hearing just the wind blow through the leaves, Hurman, feeling brave, yelled out one last remark, "Yah! I thought so! Come on, Bibole, let's get out of this dump." Strutting like he was nine feet tall, Hurman turned to walk away. "Where do you think you're going?" This voice from the darkness came. It was a voice like no other. A voice like a double-edged sword that cut through Bibole and Hurman like it was fine steel. If death had a voice, they just heard it. "Turn around. I'd like to see whom I am speaking with." Slowly turning, the two friends held on to each other for dear life. Before them on the other side of the rim stood an owl they only knew as death. He wasn't like Mr. Owl who lived on their side of the forest. This owl was young, large, and deadly. His voice was calm and confident. His talons were sharp and eager. There was no mistaking it. The two mice weren't going anywhere. "You! The big one who likes to make noise. Come closer." As he spoke those words, Hurman's body stiffened like a board. As his eyes rolled into the back of his head, feathers and bones flew up in the air as Hurman came crashing down face first at the bottom of the owl's nest. With a curious look on his face because the owl never really had a chance to ever speak to any of his meals before, he said, "Oh my, is he dead?"

Slowly looking down at his friend, Bibole, not wanting to make any sudden moves, kicked Hurman. Slowly looking up into the face of what he knew was going to be the last thing he would ever see, Bibole finally spoke, "No, he's alive, sir. He just fainted." Speaking with a voice that rang through Bibole's soul, the owl said, "How quaint! Of all nights, being the cloudiest. It's difficult to hunt when your vision is impaired by the lack of light. And just when I thought I would go without, a bat and a rat drop right into my home. Now normally, I would thank my lucky stars, but you see, I'm faced with a dilemma. Do I rip you two apart and eat you now? But then, you see, it'll spoil me. I'd expect my dinner to fall into my lap every night. You see my dilemma? A part of me says, 'Take them to the ground. Let them run a bit before adding their bones to my collection.' What to do, what to do. I know what my brother Edward would do. He'd just as soon talk you to death than eat you."

Wide-eyed, Bibole looked up. "You know Mr. Owl?" Raising one eyebrow, the owl said, "Question is, how does a bat like yourself know him?" Taking a big swallow, Bibole explained on his side of the forest, Mr. Owl was their teacher. His nephew Hoot was one of his good friends. "We play together all the time." Screaming, as if Bibole stuck a lance straight into the heart of death himself, the once-proud owl leaned over with his sharp beak pressed firmly into the chest of Bibole. "LIAR! HOW DARE YOU LIE TO ME! Owls don't play with their food!" "Oh please, sir! I'm not lying! Hoot would beg us to play with him. He said anything to get him out of the house. He feared his uncle would talk him to death. That's when we all became friends. We think Hoot is awesome! Everyone loves him and that's not a lie either . . . sir?" Raising his beak off Bibole's chest, head down and eyes closed, shaking his head, the owl spoke, "Go . . . I'm no longer hungry." Staring at the owl, Bibole's first thought was to grab his limp friend and run, run as fast and as far as he could go before the owl changed his mind. But Bibole wasn't always the first to run. Some of his friends would call that a flaw in his character while others would call that just plain crazy.

Hurman still out like a light, Bibole thought this would be a good opportunity for him to find out what was bothering this owl. It was like asking a lion why he didn't feel like eating his dinner. Head down, back turned away from his onetime meal, Bibole found himself doing the unthinkable. Slowly stretching out his hand, he placed it on the owl's wing. Startled, quickly turning his head, the owl couldn't believe his eyes. "What are you doing here? Why aren't you gone?" Shaking his head, Bibole said, "Your guess is as good as mine. I just want to know why you look so sad." Not believing what he was hearing, and the owl's ears were perfect, he asked, "Why? Why would a bat care what I'm feeling?" "It just seemed strange that when I spoke of my friend Hoot, you became very upset." Pausing for a brief moment, the owl told Bibole, "It was the eldest of our clan that would take the youngest for three of our seasons and teach them how to fly, hunt, and become perfect hunting machines so they wouldn't go hungry in life. Edward, who you called Mr. Owl, seems to have failed with the weakest of them. He failed, and now Hoot won't last through the cold seasons alone. My brother who you called teacher failed Hoot!" Bibole, eyes wide with anger, lashed out at the once-feared owl, "How can you say that? How can you say he failed? Hoot is a great friend and a great hunter! Do you know what Hoot does for fun? He likes to tease the falcons. He teases them because they can't catch him! And do you know why they can't catch him? Because your brother was teaching him a skill called AERODYNAMICS! All I know is it must work because no one can catch him, and I think maybe not even you. And who is Hoot to you anyway? Are you his guardian or something?"

A little grin came to the owl's face for a brief moment. "Yeah . . . or something." Finally turning to face Bibole, the owl sighed and said, "He's my son. My son whom I haven't seen in three seasons. My son who I'm sure has forgotten all about me." Bibole's eyes still wide open, and couldn't believe it. Because standing in front of him was a legend. A legend everyone knew as the Shadow! Still in awe, Bibole spoke up like a starstruck child meeting his hero for the first time, "You're the Shadow!" Tilting his head, not knowing what Bibole was talking about, the owl said, "What?" "The Shadow! You're the Shadow!" "Why am I a shadow?" "Not a shadow, *the* Shadow! They call you the Shadow because no one can see or hear you coming. They say you're the fastest thing in the sky. Is that true?" With a little grin, the owl said, "No. No, it's not true."

With a look of disappointment on his face, Bibole asked, "Well, what could possibly be faster than you?" Without blinking an eye and with great anticipation, Bibole stared at the sleek owl, waiting for an answer. Finally, the owl stopped grooming himself then spoke, "Light." Confused and shaking his head, Bibole asked, "Light? What about light?" With a grin, the owl said, "That's what's faster." In awe, all Bibole could say was "Awesome!" Then the owl asked, "How did I get the name Shadow?" "Your brother. He would tell stories to Hoot about his younger brother and how proud he was of you. Then Hoot would tell us. At first, we thought they were just made-up stories about a father who didn't exist. But Mr. Owl reassured us it was all true. You have a family who loves you back in our part of the woods. A family who would love to see his father, his brother, and I would be honored to take you back so you could be reunited with the ones you love."

Staring at Bibole in disbelief, the Shadow asked, "Who are you? And why is a bat so willing to help someone who was definitely at one time going to be eating them?" Slowing removing his backpack and taking off his wings, the little mouse introduced himself. "My name is Bibole, and this is my friend Hurman. He's not a rat, and I'm not a bat. We're just mice, nothing more." Slowly sitting himself down by his still-fainted friend, Bibole covered his face with his hands and slowly began to cry. Looking at Bibole's crumpled little body, the great owl leaned in, and as gently as he could, tried his best to comfort his newfound friend. "Don't worry, Bibole, I won't eat you. You're a friend of my son's, and that makes you a friend of mine." Still crying, Bibole said, "You might as well eat me. I've failed my family!" Curious, the owl replied, "Go on. It's not every day I change my mind about eating someone, then having them ask me to eat them anyway. It's a little confusing." Finally, Bibole told the owl of the three evil rats: Dr. No, Dr. Do Evil, and Dr. Feel Bad; how they kidnapped his parents; and how they were going to do something horrible to them. He told the owl how they used wings to fly above the trees so as not to be seen, wings that are now broken.

"So you see, Mr. Shadow, you might as well eat me. Those rats are too far ahead, and we'll never catch up to them, not on foot anyway." Curious and yet trying to make light of an almost impossible situation, the owl asked, "You said, 'Don't eat me.' What about your friend? I'm sure he won't feel a thing." Bursting out in tears once again, Bibole pleaded with the owl not to please eat Hurman. "He still has family, sir. But by the end of this night, I'm sure I won't. So eat me, please." Trying not to burst into laughter, the owl looked deep into the eyes of his newfound friend. "Eat you? Eat you? Just a short while ago, you said you were just mice. There's nothing *just* about you! You are the best example of what family is, and because of that, I'm going to help you get your family back." Stunned and thinking he was just being toyed with, Bibole's voice became a little stern. "That's not funny at all! In fact, it's just darn right cruel!" "Then let's stop wasting time and go get your parents back."

Silently, Bibole realized the owl wasn't toying with him. Quickly wiping the tears from his face, standing up, he humbly asked, "So what do I do?" With a grin, the owl said, "Simple. Get on." Lowering his sleek body so Bibole could climb in between the owl's wings, Bibole was told to hang on. Almost in a panic because he nearly forgot all about his friend, before taking off, Bibole yelled out, "Wait! I can't leave Hurman here!" With a quick glance behind him, the Shadow said, "Wasn't going to leave him." Snatching Hurman up with a powerful talon, before even being able to take a breath, they were gone. Holding on for dear life, Bibole couldn't believe the speed in which they were traveling, and it wasn't just the speed, it was the silence. He was truly the one called Shadow, the one everyone talked about. The one Hoot would brag about almost every week when they had their playdate. Now riding on top of this amazing beast was something to talk about. But who in all the forest would believe him? Laughing, Bibole didn't care. *So what if nobody believes me? I'll know. And that's all that's going to matter.*

Slowly opening one eye and rubbing the other, Hurman slowly started to come to. Feeling an amazing amount of wind in his face helped Hurman wake up. Clearing his eyes then his thoughts, Hurman felt the tight grip of something holding him. Hurman's hands were free, so his first thought was to try to push himself out of whatever it was that was binding him. The harder he pushed, the tighter it gripped him. When Hurman's thoughts were clear, he started to look around. Hurman's weremouse abilities were starting to come full circle. Looking straight up above him, Hurman could see the underbelly and feathers attached to what he thought, at first, was a tree trunk. All he could think about was, *How in the world did I get stuck in these roots?* But now he started to realize—realize this was his end. "Oh my gosh! What's going on?" Looking at the other talon, realizing it was empty, Hurman came to the horrible conclusion: Bibole was gone. "YOU ATE MY FRIEND! HOW COULD YOU? YOU'LL PAY DEARLY FOR THAT!" Hurman screamed at the top of his lungs. While in the tight grip of the owl, Hurman tried to think. *What can I do?* As thoughts raced through Hurman's mind, the one thought that kept coming up was . . . *I'm part weremouse! What would a weremouse do?*

Finally looking up and yelling at the owl, Hurman screamed, "You ate my friend! Now I'm going to eat you!" Biting down as hard as he could, Hurman's teeth latched on to the owl's leg. Trying to growl as he bit down, Hurman wanted to sound ferocious. Looking down, the unaffected owl calmly tilted his head and said in a matter-of-fact voice, "Your friend is trying to eat me. Would you please kindly ask him to stop? He's embarrassing himself." Biting down on the owl's leg was truly like biting a tree trunk. Hurman's teeth never stood a chance. Peeking his head out from the top, Bibole leaned over as best as he could. Watching Hurman do his very best at trying to eat the owl on behalf of his lost and departed friend made Bibole giggle a bit. Looking over the owl's wing with a big grin, Bibole yelled out, "Hey, buddy! Whatcha doing?" Looking up and seeing his lost and what he thought was his departed friend flying on the top of what Hurman still thought was death itself made him do what was to be expected—going limp once again like a rag doll. Looking down, the owl tilted his head and asked once again, "Oh my, is he dead?" Grinning from ear to ear, Bibole just shook his head and with laughter in his voice said, "No, he just fainted."

To be continued . . .

More *Adventures of Bibole, Rivol and Michelle* by Brian Fujikawa:

Book One—*The Adventures of Bibole, Rivol, and Michelle: Curse of the Weremouse*

Book Two—*The Adventures of Bibole, Rivol, and Michelle: Journey to the Forbidden City*

Book Three—*The Adventures of Bibole, Rivol, and Michelle: My Brother Pounce*

Book Four—*The Adventures of Bibole, Rivol, and Michelle: The French Fry Caper*

Book Five—*The Adventures of Bibole, Rivol, and Michelle: Kidnapped, Part One*

Book Six—*The Adventures of Bibole, Rivol, and Michelle: Kidnapped, Part Two*

Printed in the United States
By Bookmasters